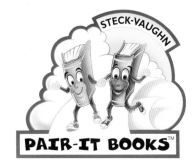

A Rainbow Bird

Written by Stephanie Handwerker

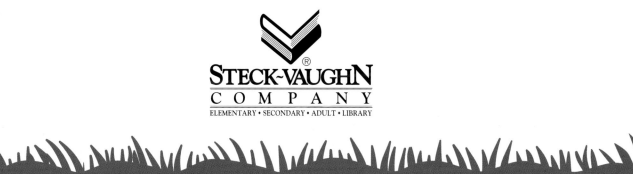

STECK-VAUGHN
C O M P A N Y
ELEMENTARY • SECONDARY • ADULT • LIBRARY

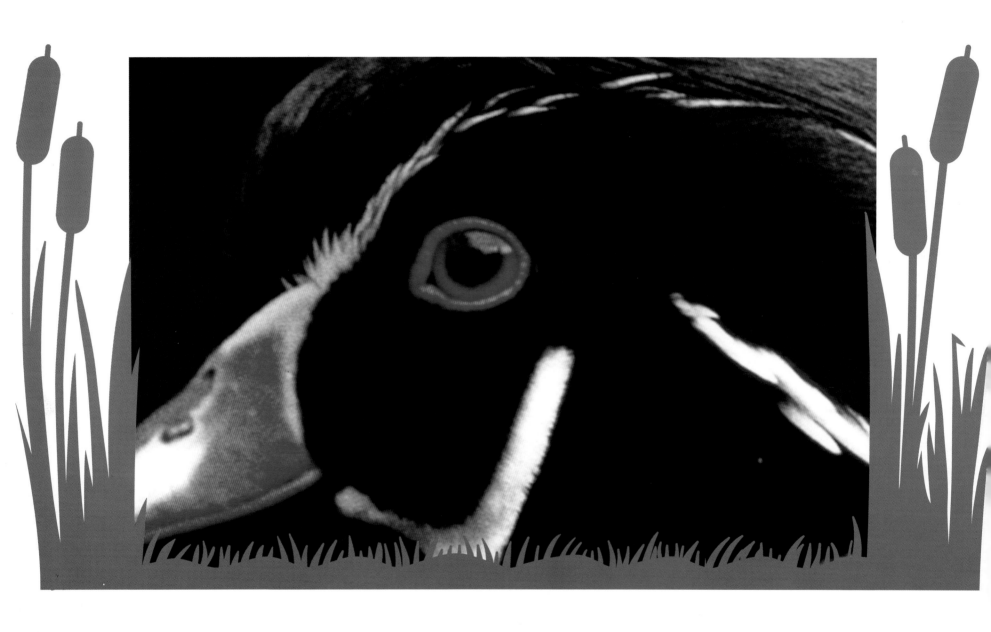

A red eye

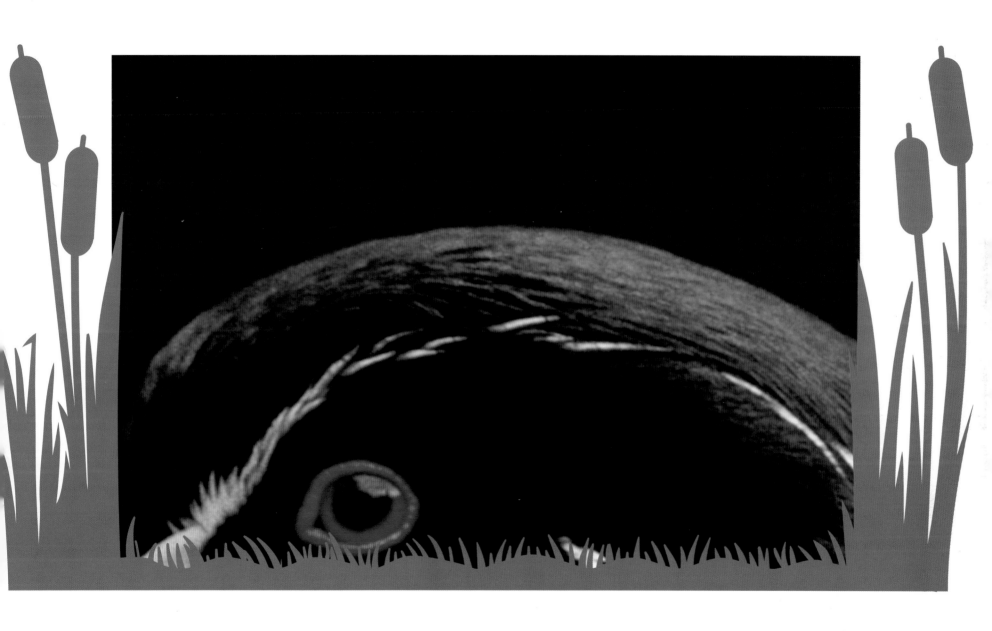

A green head

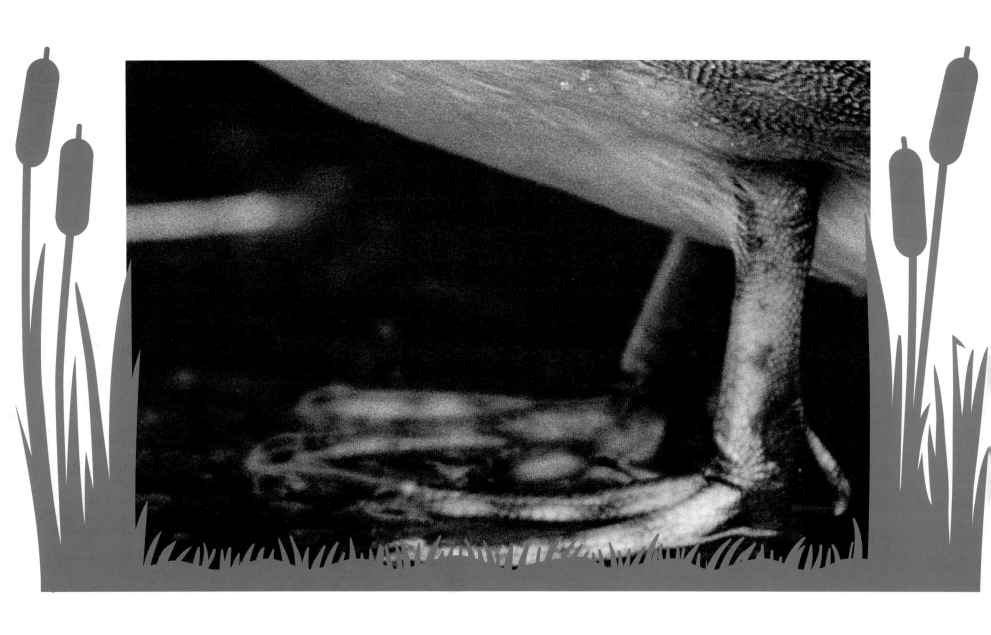

A yellow foot

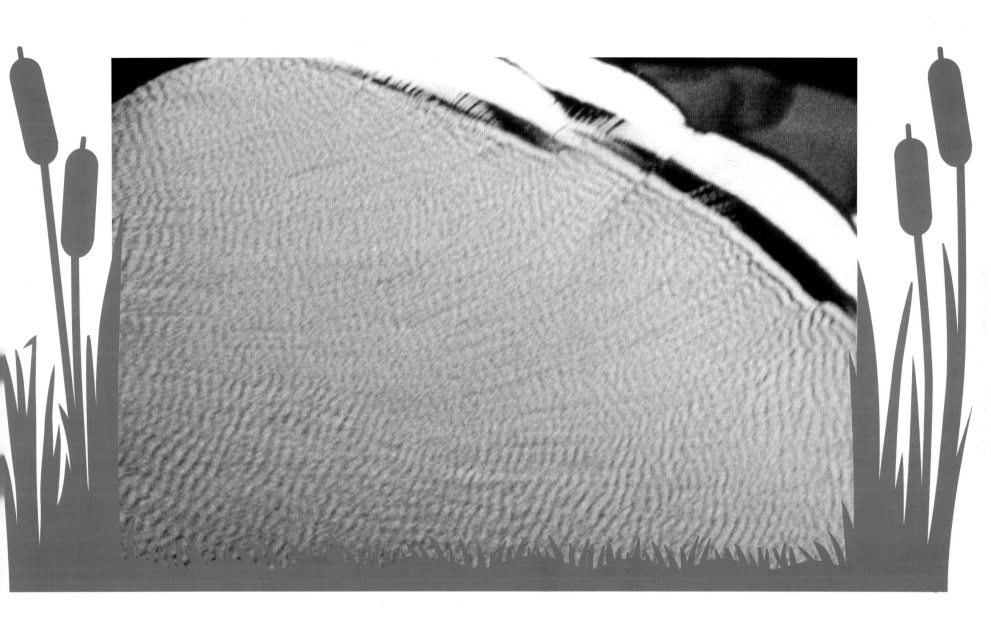

Tan feathers

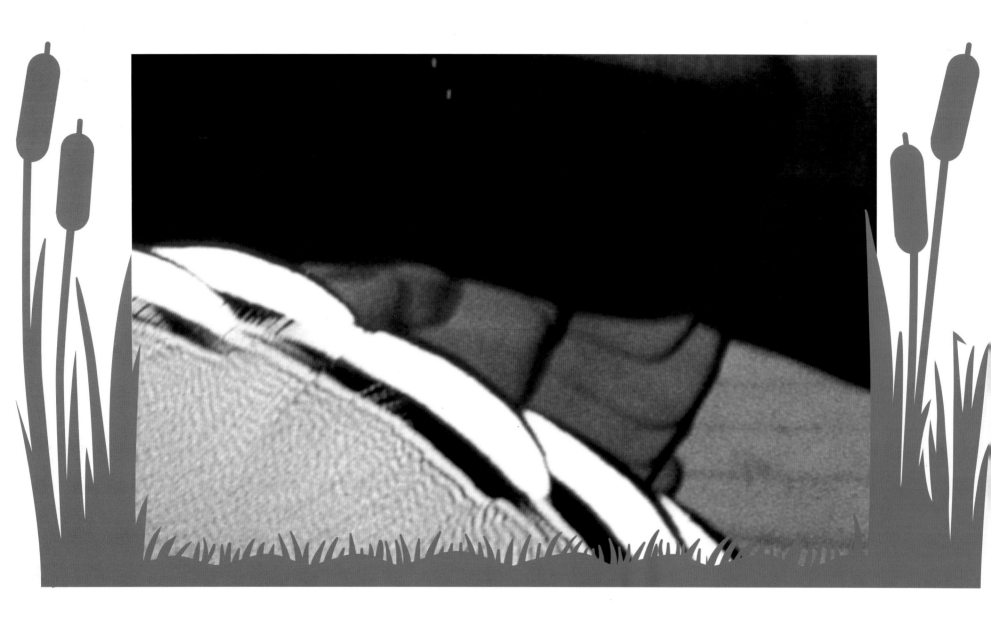

Blue feathers

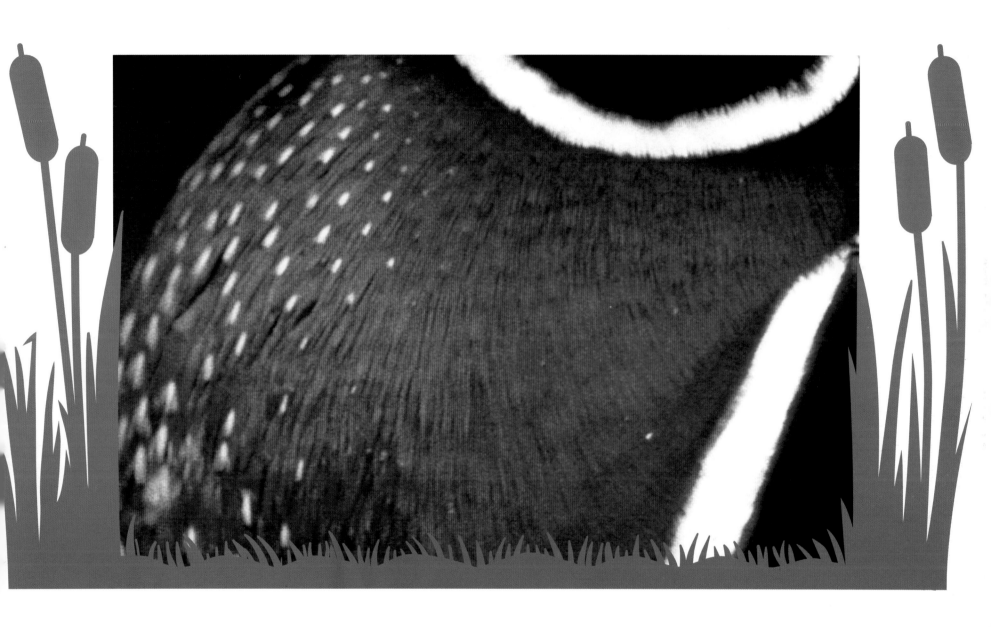

Purple feathers

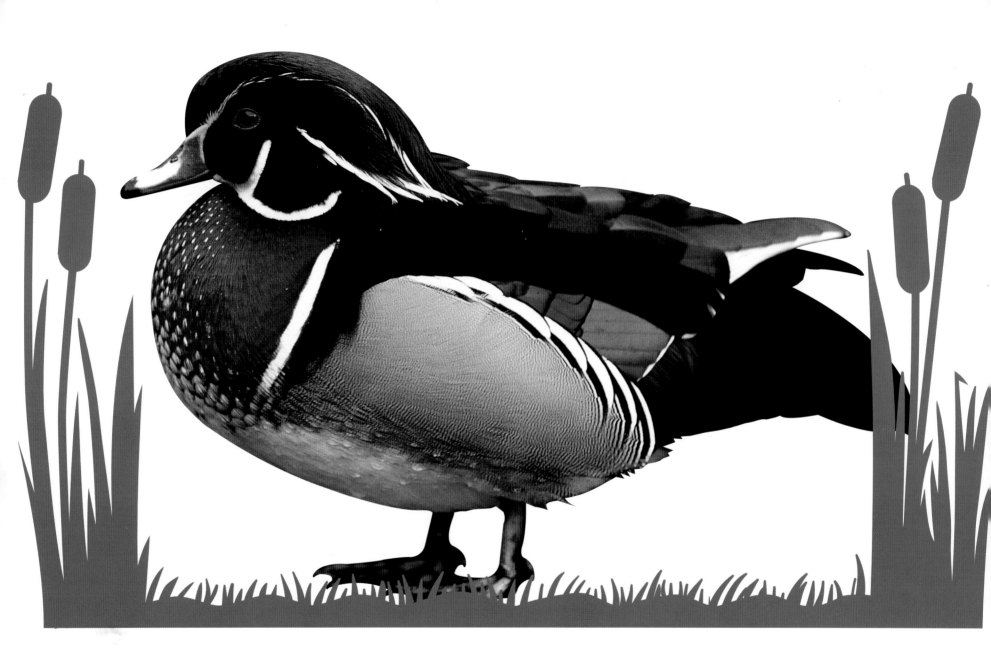

A rainbow bird